Scary hair

Written by Ian Whybrow
Illustrated by Sarah Horne

Collins

Rex was a kind dinosaur.
He liked helping other animals.

One day, his dad gave him a shop.
Dad painted the name of the shop for him –
SCARY HAIR.

His dad hoped that
Rex would eat lots
of animals.

He told Rex:
"First, they sit
in your chair.

Then you go *Raaaah!*

Then you eat them."

4

But Rex didn't want to eat animals.
He wanted to give them dinosaur haircuts.

A sad dog came to see Rex.

Pant
Pant

"I hate my name," the dog sighed.
"They call me Pants,
just because I go *pant pant*."

hair spray

Rex didn't eat the dog.
He gave him a wild dinosaur haircut.

8

"Now you can change your name to Spot!"
Rex said.

"You've made me very happy," said Spot.
"I'll tell my friend Shocker about you."

10

Shocker the sheep came along.
She said, "I hate the way I look."

Rex didn't eat her.
He cut off all her wool.

"Wow, I feel so cool!" said Shocker.
"Now I can go to a party."

Pong the skunk was too smelly to get on a bus.

He went to see Rex.
Pong said, "I hate being stinky."

15

Rex didn't eat him.
He gave Pong a wash and dry.

"Hurray!" said Pong. "Now I can go anywhere!"

Soon the shop was full of animals.
They said, "Thank you, Rex.
You've made us all very happy!"

19

"I love this job," smiled Rex.

And he painted a new name for his shop –
HAPPY HAIR!

Happy Hair

Before

After

Ideas for guided reading

Learning objectives: identify and discuss characters and how they are described in the text; predict words in sentences and investigate the sorts of words that 'fit'; know the common uses of capitalisation, e.g. names, titles, emphasis; take turns to speak, listen to others' suggestions and talk about what they are going to do

Curriculum links: Citizenship: Choices; Living in a diverse world; Taking part

High frequency words: name, that, would, first, your, then, them, want, came, call, just, because, him, now, made, very, about, way, her, off, so, us, love, new, after

Interest words: dinosaur, haircuts, scary, wild, Shocker, smelly

Word count: 243

Resources: socks, felt and wool (for puppets)

Getting started

- Show the children the book and share the title. Ask the children to guess what happens in this story, prompting them to look for clues (e.g. the scissors on the front cover).

- Introduce the main character, Rex, and ask the children to predict what kind of character he is. Ask the children to look at and read p2. *What do we know about Rex now?*

- Ask the children to read the blurb. *What do you think Rex's dad's ideas are?* Encourage the children to talk about times when they have disagreed with their carer.

Reading and responding

- As the children read aloud individually, listen in and praise strategies used to problem-solve, e.g. sounding out, blending and using context cues.

- On pp4-5, discuss Rex's dad. *What kind of character is he?*

- As they read about Rex's clients, discuss how Rex will feel after helping them.

- As individuals read, draw attention to the character's names and the fact that they all have capital letters at the start. Investigate any other capital letters used in the story e.g. the salon sign.